OUR FOREST FRIENDS

TIGER BOOKS INTERNATIONAL
LONDON

OUR FOREST FRIENDS

Nicky, a handsome fat field mouse, and his good friend Jasper, a frog, were having a lemonade at the Firling's inn in the forest. All the animals knew about the inn and to help those who did not, the Firling had hung a garland of red and blue ribbons which fluttered in the breeze. Firlings are friendly little folk who live in the forest and help look after all the animals.

"It's lovely to have such a cosy little inn to come to," said Nicky.

"I find it a bit small now," said the Firling, "as so many of my forest friends like yourselves seem to like coming here. Can you guess what I am going to do very soon?"

"Oh, don't say you are going to close down!" cried Jasper, tears coming into his eyes.

"That would be very sad," said Nicky.

"No, no, nothing like that," replied the Firling. "I would never close my inn to all my friends. I have a surprise in store for you. Come along and I'll show you!"

They followed the Firling a short way along the forest path. Very soon they came upon a clearing in a flowery patch of grass. There before them, they saw the busiest sight they had ever seen! A whole army of ants were scurrying about, building a very tall round house.

Jasper said, "Aren't they working hard! But whoever will live in such a huge house?"

"That's the surprise," said the Firling. "I am building a guest house! It will be big enough to house my friends, especially in the winter when times are hard for some of them."

Nicky and Jasper were having a lemonade at the inn.

"What a good idea!" cried Nicky. "Though there is still a lot of work to be done."

"Yes," said Jasper. "Perhaps we could do something to help."

The Firling asked his foreman, Mr. Mole, if he had a job for them. In no time at all, they found themselves busily mixing cement.

"This is fine!" cried the Firling. "It will be finished long before winter now!"

"Why not have a grand opening?" asked Jasper. "A big party for your friends!"

"Never mind about having a party," said Mr. Mole. "We'll think about one when the guest house is finished."

"Jasper, you heard what the man said," ordered Nicky. "Go and fetch the water to mix the cement."

Off Jasper trotted to the well to fill his bucket, then back again to pour it over the cement – and this went on all day long.

"My, I'm tired," said Jasper at the end of the day.

"So am I," replied Nicky, "but it will be well worth it – and we shall sleep soundly tonight."

Jasper and Nicky no sooner got into bed than they were fast asleep.

As the sun rose over the trees Jasper and Nicky woke up.

"What a good night's sleep that was," said Nicky. "Hurry up, Jasper, we've got work to do."

"Work! Work!" cried Jasper, still really half asleep.

"Yes, the guest house," said Nicky. "We've got a lot of work still to do."

"Ooooh," moaned Jasper, who although willing was not really fond of hard work.

"Stop moaning and let's have breakfast," ordered Nicky, who was feeling very hungry.

After a good breakfast of tasty bits of cheese even Jasper was

Before them was the busiest sight they had ever seen.

All the forest folk had

a happy time at the party.

ready for work on the new guest house.

All the little animals, led by Mr. Mole, worked and worked and worked. By early autumn the wonderful new guest house was finished.

"You must give it a name," said Nicky to the Firling.

"Yes, I've thought about a name," replied the Firling. "In fact, I think we should name it *The Sun*."

"Why *The Sun*?" asked Jasper.

"Because this is where all my friends will come in the winter," explained the Firling. "They will be able to keep warm, so this house will be a kind of sun."

"Can we have a party now?" asked Jasper.

"Yes," said Mr. Mole. "You have all worked very hard so you deserve to have some fun."

Everyone set about getting ready for the party. Paper lanterns were hung above the band stand as well as garlands with pretty ribbons. One of the best things was the Froggie Jazz Band. Mr. Mole danced with Freda Frog and Philip Frog with Mrs. Mouse – in fact, a joyous time was enjoyed by all the forest creatures.

In the evening all the lanterns were lit. At midnight each guest took a lantern and danced through the forest led by the Firling playing merry tunes on his fiddle.

It was one of the happiest parties the forest had ever known.

When the party came to an end, each of the guests thanked the Firling and said good-night. Nicky and Jasper went up to say their "Thank you" too.

The Firling said to them, "Why not stay with me for a while as my first guests?"

This came as a great surprise!

"Wonderful!" said Jasper, croaking with excitement.

"Oh, yes!" squeaked Nicky. He always squeaked when he became excited.

"Good! That's settled then," said the Firling.

One of their new guests was a chubby, whiskered dormouse who was very smart and handsome in a green waistcoat. His name was Chops.

Chops said, "I demand the best, you know. I would like to see where I shall sleep and what I shall eat!"

"Certainly," said the Firling. "Come to the cellar first and I will show you our winter stores."

In the cellar, Chops whistled with surprise.

"My! My!" he said. "We shan't starve. We certainly shan't starve! Tell me – does Old Man Stoat know about this cellar full of lovely food?"

"No," replied the Firling. "I never tell Old Man Stoat anything. He is not to be trusted!"

"Quite right, quite right," muttered Chops. "Why, if he did know, he would be here with those two weasels of his and clear the place out!"

"Don't worry," said the Firling, who did not seem to be bothered in the least.

At that very moment, Old Man Stoat was dashing through the forest in his cart. He cracked his whip loudly, as he sniggered slyly to himself.

"Ha! That old Firling needn't think he will keep me away from his guest house!" and again he cracked his whip. The weasels ran even faster.

"There must be a whole lot of food in that cellar and I mean to have it – yes indeed I do!"

The weasels heard, but were far too frightened to speak as the whip cracked over their heads.

Old Man Stoat called out to them, "Now listen, you two! I have a plan. I am going to steal that Firling's food and you are going to help me!"

Each guest took a lantern

and danced through the forest.

The two weasels stopped running. They listened while Old Man Stoat told them of his plan. He spoke in a low, sly voice.

"There is a tunnel at the back of that guest house that I am sure no one else knows about," he said, poking each weasel in the tummy. "You will stand guard outside the opening while I sneak down into the tunnel to get the food."

"Yes! Yes!" said both the weasels, too frightened to say

Old Man Stoat dashing through the forest.

anything else.

"When shall we do it?" asked one of the weasels.

"Soon," replied the stoat. "In fact, when there are more guests with the Firling and we won't be easily noticed."

It wasn't long before the guest house was full. Late into the evenings the Firling sat talking and laughing with his friends. Soon, everyone was sleepy and one by one went off to bed. The Firling was always the last, snuffing out the candles as he went.

Old Man Stoat had very carefully watched the guest house day after day.

"Ah, ha!" he said to himself at last. "I think the time is ripe to carry out my plan." And off he slunk to give the weasels their orders.

"You will pull the cart up to the tunnel," said Stoat in a low voice. "As soon as we are there, I will sneak down the tunnel and start carrying up all the food." He licked his lips.

"Just think of the feast! If you do your job well, I will let you have a bit of it, but just you make one mistake and you will pay for it!"

They started on their way, slinking through the long grass with Old Man Stoat in the cart behind them.

As they neared the back of the guest house, Old Man Stoat whispered, "You wait here while I creep up to see if the tunnel is still open."

Slowly, he crept through the grass. Just as he moved a branch away from the opening of the tunnel, there was a loud buzzing noise. As Stoat looked up he saw a huge swarm of bees diving towards him.

"Help! Help!" he cried, as he turned on his heels.

The Old Stoat began running for his life but the bees followed faster and faster.

This was the Firling's secret! He knew about Old Man Stoat all

A huge swarm of bees attacked the thieves.

the time and he had asked his friends the bees to make a hive there. If anyone tried to get down the tunnel, they were to attack.

And attack they did! Old Man Stoat and the weasels couldn't run fast enough.

"Oh! Oh! Help! Help!" the three of them cried.

They made a terrible noise as they all shouted together. Never again did they try to steal the Firling's winter stores – or anyone else's!

"Aren't we lucky the bees saved the winter stores?" said Chops that night. "I certainly wouldn't want to go out and look for food now." He gave a big yawn.

After that, as the days went by, the Firling's guests became sleepier and sleepier.

Then one night the Firling looked at them beside the fire and said, "It seems to me you are getting sleepier every day. Don't you think it's time you turned in for your winter sleep?"

Jasper stretched and yawned.

"I for one, am ready," he said in a lazy voice. "I am already dreaming of the spring and fresh new grass to leap about in."

"Yes, yes," said Chops sleepily. "Do let's turn in. But how shall we arrange for our food to be ready when we wake up?"

"Well," said the Firling, "I have been thinking. Why not divide it all up now? Each of you can take your share to your own room. That way, you won't have to stir until the winter is over."

In no time at all they had all the food sorted into bags with name-tags on. With a final "Sleep well!" to each other, they went upstairs to their beds.

Their beds were very snug, with lovely feather-filled covers on each. Chops was especially happy. He loved to think of all that food, right there in his room – and all for him! He carefully piled it around his bed so that he wouldn't have to reach very far when he wanted it.

They stretched and yawned ready for their winter sleep.

The Firling gets everything ready for the Christmas party.

The Firling was left to spend the winter quietly in the sleeping house. But he had work to do!

After all, there were still the birds to care for. Anyway, he must start now if everything was to be ready for their Christmas party, especially the Christmas tree which was covered with presents for all the little creatures of the forest.

Not too long after Christmas the days started to get longer and the sun warmer. Spring was on its way.

Chops with his food carefully piled around his bed.

One morning when the sun was pouring through the window Jasper stirred from his long winter sleep.

"Hurray!" shouted Jasper as he ran to look through the window. "The sun is so warm, and I expect the grass will be lovely and green. Come on Nicky! Wake up! Wake up!"

In no time at all they were dressed and dashing about the forest. They were the happiest little creatures – so happy to be alive.

In the room nearby Chops was also waking up, but he did not leap out of bed. No, he looked at all the food piled round his bed.

"My, I'm very hungry," said Chops and sat down to the biggest feast he had ever eaten!

PRINTED IN BELGIUM BY proost INTERNATIONAL BOOK PRODUCTION